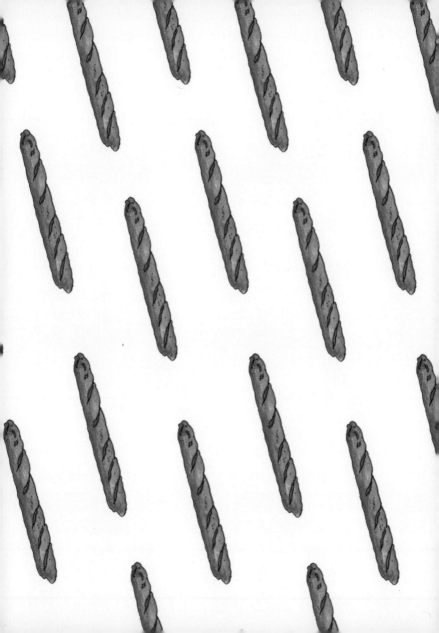

THE BAKERY OF
HAPPINESS

THE BAKERY OF
HAPPINESS

IAN BECK

Barrington Stoke

First published in 2019 in Great Britain by
Barrington Stoke Ltd
18 Walker Street, Edinburgh, EH3 7LP

www.barringtonstoke.co.uk

A CIP catalogue record for this book is available
from the British Library upon request

ISBN: 978-1-78112-878-7

Printed in China by Leo

This book is in a super-readable format for young readers
beginning their independent reading journey.

For Steven Barnham, who encouraged me to make this book, and for the boulangerie at the junction of the Rue de Prony and Rue Cardinet in Paris, where I really heard the voice

CONTENTS

Chapter 1
The Bakery

Once upon a time in Paris there was a young baker named Paul du Pain. He lived with his dog, Gracie, above his bakery shop in Paris.

His shop was in a poor part of Paris, on a corner next to some steep steps that led down to the smart areas of the city.

His customers weren't rich, but they bought bread every day, and every day Paul baked some more.

Paul started work before cock crow. He rolled and kneaded and proved and baked all through the early hours. He made crusty baguettes and rustic loaves, croissants, pains aux raisins and pains au chocolat. Every morning the delicious smell of warm bread drifted out on the air.

Paul's young assistant, Marie, arrived at seven. Gracie the dog would jump up and wag her tail when she heard Marie at the door. Marie would stroke Gracie's velvet ears every morning and say, "Silly dog". Then she would prepare the coffee and open the shop.

The sound of Marie's voice saying "Silly dog" always made Paul smile. It meant everything was right. Marie was there, which always made his heart beat a little faster, and the day could begin.

First in were the children on their way to school. Each had just a few coins to spend on treats for their lunch. Marie knew all their names and would call out "*Bonjour*" to each of them as they arrived.

"Bonjour, Françoise!"

"Bonjour, Charlotte!"

"Bonjour, Phillipe!"

"Bonjour, Salima!"

"Bonjour, Annick!"

Every morning the children left the bakery as if they had wings on their shoes and were walking on air.

*

So it went – day after day, week after week, month after month.

Paul worked hard and daydreamed that one day he'd take Marie out to the cinema. Marie greeted the customers and sold the bread, coffee and croissants. *Maybe one day Paul will ask me out*, she thought to herself. Gracie the dog just dozed and dreamed of tummy rubs and ear strokes on her cushion behind the counter.

Everyone loved Paul's bakery. People talked about what a good baker he was. His baguettes were crusty on the outside but soft and warm on the inside. His croissants were perfect and his pains au chocolat melted in your mouth. But there was something more than that. Something else that made the bakery feel magical.

Every customer always left a little
happier than when they had gone in.

Chapter 2
The Visitor

Then, one cold, wet autumn morning ...

A man came round the corner where Paul's bakery stood. As he stopped to put up his umbrella, a group of noisy schoolchildren tumbled out of the shop.

"*Bonjour, Monsieur*," Marie sang out. The man ordered a café au lait and a croissant. He took his breakfast and sat down at a table by the window. Gracie the dog got up, stretched and then came and sniffed at the bottom of the man's trousers. He was smartly dressed. He looked very important. *No crumbs or titbits here*, Gracie thought. She went and folded herself back onto her cushion with a sigh.

Rain clouds hung low over the city, but the shop was warm with the smell of fresh baking. A schoolgirl came in, and the young woman behind the counter said, "*Bonjour, Juliette!*"

Since the moment he had sat down, the important-looking man had felt happy. He felt warm and cosy and safe. He hadn't felt like that for a very long time. Was it just because the bakery was warm and dry, and outside it was cold and damp? Was it because the coffee was so good and his croissant so perfect? Or was it the smell of fresh bread?

No.

There was something else.

Something mysterious.

"*Au revoir, Juliette ...*"

There it was.

That was it.

All around him a beautiful song had been unfolding.

It was the young woman serving behind the counter. It was her voice. She didn't just speak ... she sang. She spoke in tune and had perfect pitch.

Every word was like a song.

That was why the children had left
the shop as if they were floating on air.
He felt that he was on a cloud too. This
girl had the loveliest voice he had ever
heard, and he had heard them all.

The important-looking man was
Monsieur Luc Leroux. He was the
director of the great opera house down
in the city. He knew all about singing
and singers.

He was sure he had found a new singing sensation. A future star of stars. Here she was working in a humble bakery in a poor and dingy area of Paris.

He took a deep breath. Then he went to the counter and said, "Excuse me, Mademoiselle ... Forgive me, but there is something I must ask. It is about your voice."

"My voice?" Marie said, puzzled.

"Yes, your voice. I think you have it in you to be a singer. Not just any singer but a great singer. One of the best." He took a card out of his pocket. "I am Luc Leroux," he said with a click of his heels and a bow, "of the Paris Opéra. And I am at your service, Mademoiselle."

Chapter 3
Everything Changes

In the back room, Paul was just then ready for a break. His face as always was dusted white with flour, which made him look like a circus clown. He stepped out from his kitchen and saw Marie and the important-looking man talking together.

The man was saying, "If you would kindly come to see me at the Opéra as soon as is possible, then we can begin. There is no time to lose. The world needs to hear your voice, to hear you sing."

"I don't think that I have any special talent," Marie said, blushing.

"You are wrong, Mademoiselle," the man said. "A talent like yours must be shared with the world."

"Talent, Monsieur?" Paul asked. He began to feel alarmed that his happy life was about to change.

"Yes, great talent. Have you never noticed Mademoiselle's voice?" said Monsieur Leroux.

"Well, yes," Paul said as he rubbed his floury hands on a tea towel, "there is something special about her voice."

"More than something," Monsieur Leroux said. "I have never heard better. I have asked Mademoiselle ..." He stopped and turned to Marie. He didn't even know her name.

"Marie Moulin," Marie said.

"I have asked Mademoiselle Moulin
to come to the Opéra as soon as possible.
I see a golden future for her."

"A golden future," Paul said. "How do
you feel about that, Marie?"

"I think I am a little excited, although
I can't really believe it," Marie said.

"You hear that voice?" Monsieur
Leroux said. "Musical magic."

Paul nodded. "I do not wish to stand in your way, Marie," he said. "You do not have to work for me. You are, of course, free to leave at any time."

Monsieur Leroux said, "I don't want to rush you, Mademoiselle, but we have a new season beginning in a few weeks. We need a new star and I think you are that star! You are the person we need!" Then he turned to Paul, "May I use your telephone?"

"I have no telephone," Paul said, and he pointed to the street outside, "but there is a telephone cabinet – there at the top of the steps."

"I shall telephone for a taxi, and by the way, Monsieur, your coffee and croissants are excellent."

Gracie came to see what the fuss was about. Paul stroked her ear. "We shall miss you, Marie, won't we, Gracie?"

Marie stroked Gracie's other ear and said, "Silly dog. I shall miss you too, but I will come and see you both. I promise."

*

The taxi arrived and took Monsieur Leroux and Marie away.

That afternoon, Paul wrote a sign which said the shop needed a new assistant. As he stuck it in the window, he felt sad. Why had he never asked Marie out to the cinema? He wished he had. Now it was too late. Would he ever see her again? Gracie the dog came and leaned against him, and they both looked out at the rain together.

Chapter 4
Missing Marie

Marie became famous.

There were adverts for her shows in the newspaper, and once Paul even saw Marie's face on a poster stuck on the side of a bus.

Paul baked and daydreamed of going to see Marie sing at the Opéra.

Gracie slept on her cushion behind the counter and dreamed of Marie stroking her ears.

Lucie, Paul's new assistant, was nice enough, but she wasn't sure about Gracie the dog and was too shy to stroke any ears.

The customers all left the bakery feeling just the same as when they went in. The children set off for school with their feet firmly on the ground. There was no more spring in their step. No more wings. Not as many people came now for their morning coffee. They all missed Marie. They missed the sound of her nightingale voice as she called out her greetings and their names. Paul looked pale and sad.

*

While Paul baked day after day, Marie sang at the Opéra.

Day after day, week after week, month after month.

Night after night, the people at the Opéra cheered and clapped for Marie. Her fans threw flowers onto the stage. Crowds waited for her autograph. There were posters of her all over Paris.

One evening, Paul passed her picture when he walked Gracie. The dog stopped and looked sadly at the picture.

"We really must go and see Marie," Paul said. "You miss her, don't you?"

"Woof!" Gracie agreed, and wagged her tail.

At last, one evening they went to the Opéra. But there were no tickets left. It was sold out that night and for weeks ahead.

It started to rain.

"Oh dear, that was silly," Paul said to Gracie. "I should have booked tickets and I forgot to bring the umbrella. We'll wait here by the stage door and try to see Marie after the show."

They sheltered from the rain across the road in the doorway of a flower shop. A crowd built up as the evening passed. They all had umbrellas, so Paul and Gracie could hardly see the stage door.

Suddenly, there was a burst of excited chatter.

"Here she comes," somebody called out.

"Magnificent Marie," called somebody else.

The umbrellas all pushed forward. They pushed against Paul and Gracie.

Paul and Gracie had to stand away from the crowd back out in the rain again.

They couldn't see Marie – there were too many people and too many umbrellas.

Chapter 5
Clever Dog

But Gracie wasn't going to give up. As the umbrellas all pushed forward, she pulled free of Paul and slipped out of her lead. She ran into the crowd.

"Hey, Gracie!" Paul shouted as he pushed after her. "Come back!"

As the crowd moved out of the way for Gracie, Paul saw Marie. She was leaning forwards, and he heard her say "Silly dog" as she stroked Gracie's ear. Gracie's tail spun round and round, and Paul's heart turned over once again, as it always had.

Paul stood in front of Marie, his hair wet, looking as sad as the dog was happy.

"Sorry, Marie, she got away from me," he said.

"I've missed her," Marie said, and stroked Gracie's wet but happy head some more.

"She sits at the door at seven every morning to look out for you," Paul said.

"Silly dog," Marie said, and then, "Look at you, you're both soaking wet."

"I know," Paul said. "I forgot to bring my umbrella."

"You need looking after, doesn't he, Gracie?" Marie said.

"We'd better go," Paul said. "Early to bed and the early bread will rise. Good to see you looking so happy, Marie."

"I will come and see you both soon, I promise," Marie said, and her words sounded to Paul like a sad song. He walked away with Gracie, and as they climbed the steep steps back to the bakery the rain stopped at last. "Well, that's one good thing," Paul said.

Chapter 6
A Surprise Visitor

Days went by. Weeks went by.

Paul rolled and kneaded and proved and baked. Gracie sat at the door at seven every morning to wait for Marie. But, instead, it was always the new girl, Lucie. She was friendly but still shy, and she wasn't Marie.

Then one bright morning, Paul was working at the oven when he heard a voice he knew sing out, "Silly dog". There was an excited bark from Gracie. The customers began to clap and cheer. Marie was back.

There she was, wearing very fine clothes and smiling while she stroked the dog's ears.

"The bread smells as lovely as ever, Paul," she said.

Paul nodded. "Thank you," he said. "I do my best."

"I miss the bakery, you know," she said, "even the early-morning starts in cold weather."

Paul nodded.

"I don't sing at the Opéra every evening, as that would be bad for my voice," Marie went on. "So do you think I might come back here and serve the customers sometimes? On the days when I'm not singing?"

"Well," Paul said, his heart racing, "that would be lovely, but I am not sure I can afford two assistants."

"You wouldn't have to pay me at all," said Marie. "I just miss my old life and the people here, and of course this silly dog. I would love to be part of it all again if I could."

*

So it was that on the next bright morning, the children arrived to buy their lunch-time treats and they heard their names sung out by a familiar voice.

"Bonjour, Françoise!"

"Bonjour, Charlotte!"

"Bonjour, Phillipe!"

"Bonjour, Salima!"

"Bonjour, Juliette!"

"Bonjour, Annick!"

The children left the bakery smiling and once more flew down the steps as if their feet had wings.

Every customer felt better for hearing Marie's voice again, and the word spread that Marie Moulin, Magnificent Marie herself, could sometimes be found serving coffee and croissants in a humble baker's shop.

Paul's business did better and better.
At last, he plucked up the courage to
ask Marie if she would like to go to
the cinema with him. She smiled and,
after stroking Gracie's velvet ears, said,
"Yes, of course," and her reply sang
out like magical music among the cups
and plates and the smell of fresh warm
bread.

Our books are tested
for children and young people by
children and young people.

Thanks to everyone who consulted on
a manuscript for their time and effort in
helping us to make our books better
for our readers.